ELEVEN ROSES
AND OTHER STORIES
By
David Wood

Drawings by Ted Schultz, a lifer, a friend.

ETERNAL WANDERER PRESS
P. O. Box 55452
St. Petersburg, FL 33732
dmw.13@netzero.net
pawsore@netzero.net
eiryu113144@yahoo.com
huntertrilogy@yahoo.com

This book is dedicated to Dona Payne,

My oldest friend,

My bestest friend,

My dearest friend,

Who never gave up on me

When I was in my darkest state.

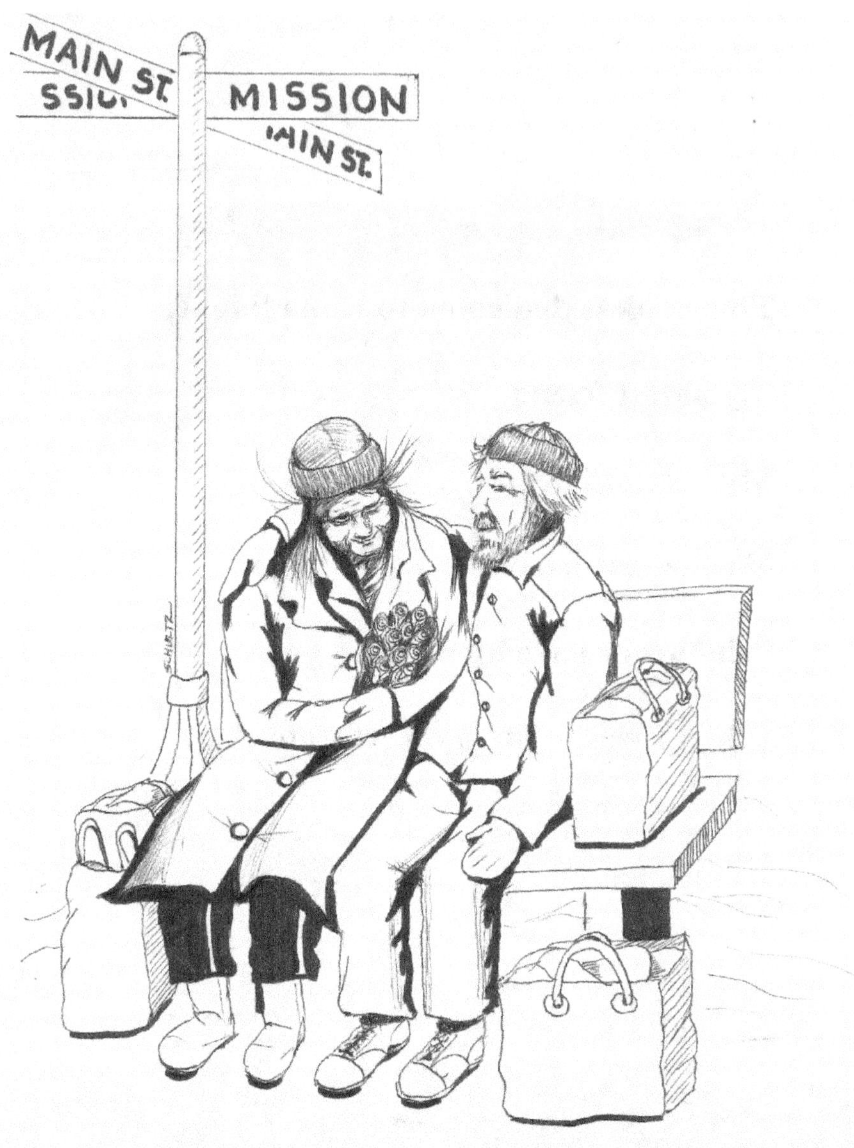

MAIN ST.
MISSION
MAIN ST.

INTRODUCTION:

I have been writing since I was around twelve or thirteen, and though I have never reached the state where I became rich or famous, I did find pleasure in the things I wrote, and I never regretted it.   Writing is both an escape from the world and myself and a self-analysis of myself and the world, a chance to create and write down events and feelings, to make characters from what little I know of the human condition, to begin and complete a process of creativity that I have always envied from the first short story of poem I ever read.

I could never honestly say I am a good writer, but I am a writer, and that is enough for me. I spent maybe a year or two writing the first and second paragraphs of what I thought was a great story only to stop and never come back to that page.   At the age of thirteen, I finished a one page "essay" about my homeroom class, called 7-5, Class of the Year!"   What bullshit.   But it was the first time I ever finished something I started writing, and it was the catalyst I needed to go on from there.

As long as I have been writing, I still barely understand the process, but any time another writer asks for my advice, I always say: (1) READ.   And (2) WRITE.   By reading, you wither consciously or subconsciously pick up the style of the writer and you are able to decide what style you like best.   And you write as much as you can, never worrying how bad it is.   If all you do is write shit, then write shit. If you stick with it long enough, you might just write your first gem.

I am not sure if what I am presenting to you now is shit or gems (or maybe just rhinestones) but I like them, and I feel like sharing them. So, for now, enjoy these pieces, dear reader, and I hope you find a few gems among them.

---David Wood

ELEVEN ROSES

John Martin "Sonny" Preston flattened his large, red, bulbous nose against the Kaufmann's showcase window, watching the mechanical elves inside make toys in a fantasy Santa's shop.

"I just gotta get her something," he told them, his breath fogging the glass. He turned and yanked his thick, dirty blue pullover cap tighter over his long, gray hair. Large snowflakes floated to the streets, slushy from traffic.

Streetlights revealed sooty snow along the sidewalks. It was Christmas Eve, and few pedestrians were left, save for a couple of small lines outside movie theaters. Christmas music reverberated off the walls of old skyscrapers, following Sonny as he hurried on.

A taxi passed, splashing slush onto the icy sidewalk, but Sonny ignored it as he spotted Ginny Anne Marlowe in the line for the Christian Ladies' Shelter. Ginny was massive in her coats, each arm grasping a tattered garbage bag full of all her worldly treasures.

"Ho! Ginny!" Sonny shouted, waving a gloved hand as he rushed up to her.

"Ah, Sonny," she said, laughing through a toothless grin. "Ah, Sonny, I can't talk now, Sonny. I gotta get in here and get my bed, you know."

"Ginny," Sonny said, "Whatcha want for Christmas?"

"Ah, Sonny," she laughed, and Sonny laughed too, her laughter was so infectious. "Ah, Sonny, I want a million bucks and a big car, and a . . ."

"I mean, really," Sonny asked. "For real."

"For real?" Ginny asked, flakes of snow in her brownish-gray hair. "Ah, Sonny, ain'tcha sweet. But Ginny takes care of Ginny, ya know."

"Yeah, well, tomorrow is Christmas," Sonny said, scratching his whiskers, "and . . . well . . ."

"Ah, Sonny, you're so sweet," Ginny said, almost glowing with warmth. The line started moving again, the other women stepping forward passively. Only Ginny, with her garbage bags, was animated. "You know what I'd like?" she shouted at the entrance. "I'd like a big, red, long-stemmed rose." Then she was gone.

"A rose?" Sonny asked. "A rose in winter?" But the door to the Christian Ladies' Shelter was closed.

Sonny got his own bed at the Brother Billy Bob's Soup, Soap and Hope Mission, where the soup was watery, the bread was hard, but the coffee was thick and steamy and ran until bedtime. Brother Bill's sermon about lost sheep was short, followed by plenty of gospel songs from the tattered hymnals. Sonny slept with his socks under one arm and the Ace bandages he used to wrap his stockinged feet under the other arm so they'd be dry by morning. His Christmas Day breakfast consisted of coffee, burned toast and greasy, fried potatoes, another sermon, then back on the street.

The morning light reflected blindingly off the freshly fallen snow. Most stores were closed, but a few would be open until noon. Sonny set off walking, grumbling to himself. "A rose in winter . . ."

He found three flower shops that were open, but none of them had roses. He had been walking for two hours already, and his socks were soaked, and his toes numb with cold. The sky was no longer blue, but overcast, and snow had begun falling again.

"A rose in winter," Sonny growled, his thick, gray eyebrows knitting together like two woolly caterpillars in a pas-de-deux. Then he recalled all the times Ginny made him laugh, and he grinned, feeling new energy.

He found roses at Floral Designs — they had a dozen left, but they cost $5 apiece. Sonny rummaged through his pocket and came up with 47 cents. The warmth of the brightly lighted store and the smell of chemical fertilizer and flowers followed him as he went out the door. He wandered, looking at store windows with grates across them to discourage burglary. He saw a pawnshop that was open and recalled the old wedding ring he pawned years ago.

Then, looking across the street at a Gimbels entrance, he saw a thin man in a Santa suit with a fake beard and a real bell. He was standing by a plastic cauldron supported by a tripod advertising some charity. Sonny watched as departing shoppers dropped loose change into the cauldron.

Going into the alleyway, Sonny came up with a Campbell's soup can. He then went to another entrance of the building, where he held the can with both gloved hands, shouting, "Coins for the poor! Coins for the poor!" The passing shoppers wouldn't look at him, but dropped loose change into his can. It was just gaining weight when the Santa's brass bell bounced painfully off his head.

"Git outta here!" Santa yelled, shaking his fist. "This is my territory! Yer messin' with my customers!" Sonny scooped up the dropped coins from the snow and ran off, still hearing Santa's ravings a block away.

He arrived at Floral Designs, walking up to the counter with his change.

"I'd like a red, long-stemmed rose," he said, rubbing his head where the bell hit him, "but I'm a little short."

The woman counted the change he dropped on the counter, then shook her head. "I'm sorry," she said, "but if you would like a chrysanthemum."

"Oh, no," Sonny said, "but maybe I could scape together the money in another hour."

'We close in five minutes," the woman said.

Sonny looked at her with pleading eyes.

The woman shook her head.

Sonny sighed, sliding his coins off the counter into a gloved hand. He went outside and stood in the falling snow. Other stores were closing. It was Christmas Day, after all. A recorded choir sang through outdoor speakers, "Hark! The herald angels sing . . ."

He counted his change again, as though he expected the amount to magically increase. A man stepped out of Floral Design carrying a dozen red roses wrapped in delicate pick tissue paper. The dozen roses! Sonny thought to himself in panic.

He walked after the man. "Hey, mister!" The man saw him and started walking faster. "Wait! Please!"

The man stopped and spun around. "What do you want?"

"I'd like to buy one of your roses."

"Do I look like a flower shop to you?" the man snapped. "These are for my wife."

"Sir, listen: I have a friend, and it's Christmas and I already tried to buy her a rose, but I only have three dollars and change."

"And I'm supposed to care?" the man grumbled. Sonny just stared. The man looked away. "Oh, hell," the man grumbled, gently removing one rose from the dozen, a piece of baby's breath hooked to a thorn. "It's Christmas, I guess."

Sonny took it very carefully in dirty-gloved fingers, then handed out the change. "Keep it," the man said. "I just hope my wife doesn't notice there are only 11 roses."

"Just give her one," Sonny said. "Women think one long-stemmed rose is very romantic."

"And who made you an expert?" the man grumbled.

"Why do you think I only wanted one?" Sonny said. The man tilted his head, then looked at his roses.

Later, on a park bench, Sonny handed Ginny 11 roses. Ginny's toothless grin was never so wide. "But ain't they expensive?" She smelled them. "And so many."

"I would've had 12," Sonny said, "but a man needed one for his wife. And you know how it is — Christmas and all." Ginny crushed him with a hug. "I got some change. Wanna look for a burger?"

"Ah, Sonny," Ginny said. "Ya didn't have to."

"Merry Christmas, Ginny."

"Roses in winter," Ginny said. "It just makes everything so alive." She hugged him again, kissed his bulbous nose. "Ah, Sonny! Merry Christmas!"

The other street people saw them later, Ginny carrying her roses like they were a baby, and Sonny carrying her garbage bags. They were looking for a fast-food place that might be open. The snow fell, and Christmas music flowed through the streets.

"Keep it," the man said. "I just hope my wife doesn't notice there are only 11 roses."

"Just give her one," Sonny said. "Women think one long-stemmed rose is very romantic."

"And who made you an expert?" the man grumbled.

"Why do you think I only wanted one?" Sonny said. The man tilted his head, then looked at his roses.

Later, on a park bench, Sonny handed Ginny 11 roses. Ginny's toothless grin was never so wide. "But ain't they expensive?" She smelled them. "And so many."

"I would've had 12," Sonny said, "but a man needed one for his wife. And you know how it is — Christmas and all." Ginny crushed him with a hug. "I got some change. Wanna look for a burger?"

"Ah, Sonny," Ginny said. "Ya didn't have to."

"Merry Christmas, Ginny."

"Roses in winter," Ginny said. "It just makes everything so alive." She hugged him again, kissed his bulbous nose. "Ah, Sonny! Merry Christmas!"

The other street people saw them later, Ginny carrying her roses like they were a baby, and Sonny carrying her garbage bags. They were looking for a fast-food place that might be open. The snow fell, and Christmas music flowed through the streets.

TUESDAY'S SCENARIO

Mickey Stouthead stood naked and shivering at the foot of the double bed. Gloria Radcliffe, with the bedclothes just covering her ample breasts, smiled mischievously at him, beckoning him to her side. Over 20 years his senior, Gloria was absolutely sensual; none of the college girls in his sophomore classes held a candle to her. As Mickey stepped to the side of the bed, eager to fulfill his "Mrs. Robinson" fantasy, Gloria gestured for him to wait. "Let's turn these lights off first, shall we?"

"The lights?" Mickey said, surprised. "Yeah. The lights. Sure." He reached over and flicked the switch, throwing the room into darkness. Gloria's modesty was annoying. She had made him undress in the bathroom while she crawled under the covers. Then again, they'd been dating every Tuesday night for three months before she finally invited him to her one-story home. But Mickey didn't care how eccentric she was. He groped in the darkness until he found the covers, anticipating her body next to his. As he lifted the sheets, he heard the front door open.

"Uh-oh," Gloria said.

"What was that?" Mickey asked.

"My husband," Gloria answered.

"Holy shit!" Mickey gasped as he flipped the lights back on. "Where's the back door?"

"Left and down the hall," Gloria said.

Mickey opened the bedroom door and dashed out, then rushed back in. "My clothes!" he shouted, rushing into the bathroom. He returned with his bundle and sat on the foot of the bed as he pulled his socks on.

"Arthur!" Gloria gasped.

"Gloria!"

Mickey dropped his tennis shoe. Arthur, Gloria's husband, stood stiff and red-faced in the bedroom doorway. With a gray crew cut, thin jowls, and sunken eyes, Arthur looked like the Grim Reaper might look in a three-piece suit. "Ohhh . . ." Mickey groaned.

"Gloria, what's the meaning of this?"

"Arthur, don't get mad, I . . ."

"I'm getting my gun!" Arthur shouted. "Where's my gun?"

That was all Mickey had to hear. He gripped his bundle of clothes to his chest and shoved past Arthur. "Scuse me," he said and ran down the hall. In the kitchen, he found the back screen door jammed shut. He heard a blast behind him and the window next to him splintered apart. Arthur had found his gun.

Without waiting for the next shot, Mickey leaped through the screen door and ran down the sidewalk.

Mickey was going his fastest while keeping his head low. He heard two more shots and suddenly remembered a childhood prayer. He raised his head and glanced back to see if Arthur had stopped. He had, at least long enough to aim. Mickey leaped to the left as he heard another shot.

The streets were deserted at that time of night, but Mickey saw people through the back door of the Frisky Lady Nightclub. He rushed through the door without looking back.

The doorman would have asked for identification but he was too surprised that Mickey wore nothing but socks. Mickey rushed along the back walkway behind the crowd, thankful that the lights were low. The patrons were preoccupied by the band, "The Decapitated Rhinos." The drummer spotted Mickey and froze in mid-beat.

Rushing out the front door and back on the street, Mickey kept running, rushing from the glare of one street light and another. He stopped at the corner and glanced around. Somebody yelled something obscene from a passing car. Mickey gasped for breath and tried balancing on one leg as he pulled on his pants. He heard another shot behind him. "Holy shit!" he gasped, dropping all but his pants and running across the street.

At the next intersection, he spotted a red Mustang waiting for the traffic light to change. "Stuart!" he shouted and ran to the car. Stuart Weaver leaned over and rolled down the passenger side window. Mickey grabbed the car door. "Stuart, you gotta help me!"

"Hey, Michael," Stuart said, raising an eyebrow.

"Stuart, there's a killer following me!"

"Well, you'd better put some clothes on, Mickey," Stuart said, noticing the pants in Mickey's hand.

Mickey tried the door, but it wouldn't open. He looked back and saw Arthur, who had just finished reloading his gun and was now taking a Clint Eastwood stance as he aimed. Mickey leaped head first into the window, getting stuck halfway. "Drive," he shouted, trying to get his dangling legs pulled in. "Drive, dammit!"

"Hey, man, it's a red light!"

"Just drive!" Mickey shouted as he tumbled into the car.

"Hey, Mickey, would you put your pants on, man?" Stuart said.

Suddenly the rear window exploded inwards, spitting glass against their heads and shoulders. "Jee-zus!" Stuart screamed, flooring the gas pedal. The Mustang leaped forward, darting in front of a Peterbilt 18-wheeler. The Peterbilt swerved into another lane to avoid hitting the

Mustang, but its load refused to change lanes and dozens of apple crates went crashing to the pavement.

Mickey glanced through the back window, watching the figure of Gloria's husband disappear in the distance. He turned to Stuart, whose knuckles were turning white on the steering wheel. "Hey, thanks for the lift, Stu." He forced a smile.

Stuart quickly glanced at him without moving his head, then glanced back at the road. "No problem, man," he said. "Long time no see, huh?"

"Yeah," Mickey said, pulling his pants on. "You got some heat in this car?"

"Not when the back window's blown out, man," Stuart said. "But the radio still works." He had finally slowed down to the speed limit before stopping at the next red light and looking over his shoulder. "Who's your friend?"

Mickey zipped up his pants. "You remember that lady I've been dating every Tuesday night?"

"Oh, yeah, man," Stuart grinned. "She's a fox."

"Well, that's her husband."

"Oh," Stuart said, driving on when the light turned green. "I didn't know you went out with married woman."

"Neither did I," Mickey sighed. "I was wondering why she would see me only on Tuesday nights. She'd always call me, but I couldn't call her, you know? I should've figured she was married or something, Stu. I need a beer."

"So do I," Stuart nodded. "We can earn a couple good hangovers tonight, man. What with no morning classes, we've got it made."

"Yeah, I need to get drunk tonight! And you can bet I'll never see that Gloria again. No, wait, I can't."

"Can't stop seeing Gloria?"

"Can't get drunk," Mickey slapped his forehead. "I have a meeting tomorrow at eight. I signed on as a subject for a psychological profile. Somebody wants to study stress on college students who face unusual situations."

"Well, hell," Stuart said, offering Mickey a cigarette. "What's so unusual about your life?"

"Who knows?" Mickey lit the cigarette. "But they paid me $500 when I signed up some time ago, so why ask. I would've forgotten about tomorrow's meeting, but the secretary called me up this morning."

"You could still use a couple of pitchers," Stuart said. "By the way, did you and Gloria . . . ?"

"Nah," Mickey shook his head. "Tonight would have been the first time. Only her husband walked in on us. Talk about bad timing!"

*   *   *   *   *

"Talk about great timing!" Gloria said. "You walked in just in time. Mickey was about ready to jump all over me."

Arthur was wheezing, leaning against the bedroom wall, his clothes wet from the rain. "He'll jump tomorrow when he sees me at his psychological profile." He grinned. "The experiment went well. Tomorrow . . ." he puffed, "tomorrow we'll have the results." He admired his wife, who smiled back at him, then took a drag on her cigarette. The one-piece strapless bathing suit she wore was perfect for the illusion of being naked under the covers. "He gave me a run for my money," Arthur wheezed, "but it was worth it."

"But did you have to use real bullets?"

"It was more dramatic that way," Arthur said. "Better for research." He opened a dresser drawer and put his gun away. "Besides, I'm a marksman and nobody got hurt."

"Just be sure you use blanks tomorrow night." Arthur thought about it. "I think you're right," he said, pulling a folded piece of paper out of his shirt pocket. "Let's see. Monday's scenario: husband comes home, finds wife and wife's lover, and has a heart attack. Tuesday's scenario: husband comes home, finds wife and wife's lover, and tries to shoot the lover. Wednesday's scenario: husband comes home, finds wife and wife's lover, and shoots wife . . .Yes, blanks it is!"

SCHULTZ

THE MAN WHO LIVED IN THE CELLAR

When I first met Peter Monk, I thought he was the perfect resident for the cellar apartment. His clothes were like ancient drapes or Salvation Army counter rejects; his hair was a lawn gone to weed; his glasses were a jigsaw puzzle of cracked lenses and frame held together by super glue and masking tape. Like the cellar, he was a collection of flotsam and jetsam.

But what really brought him to my attention was his accusation that Mrs. Hedley, our landlady, came from another planet.

One could locate Peter's room by way of a path that went from the cellar steps to his door, then arched back through the storage boxes to the washer and dryer. My apartment was on the third floor, but I got to know him on my laundry days. To Peter, the cellar was like a horn of plenty. He was always inventing marvelous appliances from the cellar junk

"Lookit this," he would say, holding up an ancient toaster that suddenly played music. "Couldn't get it to toast anymore, so I made it into a radio."

"Nice," I would say, giving him an odd look. There were plenty of broken radios in the cellar he could have repaired, but I guessed he was saving them to make toasters.

Nonetheless, I was really amazed at his mechanical and electrical abilities, and sometimes, I was even thankful for them. For instance, not only did he soup-up my old Volkswagen "Bug," he also built a "fuzz-buster" radar detector out of an electrical toothbrush and parts of a microwave oven. I made some classical runs in the old Bug after that, with no fear of being caught speeding!

One morning he woke me from a pleasant dream. He was in a near-panic. He was standing in my bedroom, holding my clothes. "You have to help me," he insisted. "C'mon, get dressed."

"How did you get in?" I asked, shading my eyes.

"I picked the lock, but that's not important." He adjusted his glasses, which were sagging at the bridge. "There has been an intergalactic crisis on the planet Zen-Thombe, and I have to make contact with a fleet of starships as they pass Earth!"

I blinked my eyes. "Would you kindly repeat that, but slower?"

"Trust me," he insisted. "Zen-Thombe has been attacked, and some other planet will soon be invaded. We have to find out which planet, and stop the invasion."

Still not quite awake, I moved my face closer to his and sniffed his breath. If he was on anything, he must have snorted it. "Look," I said, "everybody's entitled to their own beliefs and persuasions, but enough is enough." I flopped back on my pillow. "And please lock the door on your way out."

"Please!" Peter moaned, flapping his arms. "I really need your help! You can't let me down!"

I opened one eye. I knew I wasn't going to get rid of him. "All right," I said, opening the other eye and taking my clothes. "What do I have to do?"

The supermarket wasn't open that early, but there were several grocery carts in the parking lot. We confiscated two of them, then headed across town with the cartwheels squeaking all the way. As we headed through a park, Peter pointed to a grassy mound. It was six feet high, and thirty feet in diameter, near a set of swings. "Mrs. Hedley's spaceship is buried under there," Pete told me.

I frowned and mumbled, "Don't press your luck, Pete."

We arrived at the Sony shop by ten, bringing the carts in with us. Peter immediately began dragging the salesclerk around, buying television sets, radios, video sets, stereos and satellite parts. He produced a MasterCard, complete with identification for Mr. John Grenthrew, whose driver license photo looked remarkably like Pete.

We filled the carts, but made several more stops on the way home. With other credit cards, and with other names, Peter bought two user-friendly computers, copper plumbing pipe, a thousand feet of thick cable, a kitchen sink disposal unit, and two arcade video games. Arranging for most of it to be delivered within the hour, we pushed the carts back, and unpacked at the cellar door.

That afternoon was hectic. We were putting strange things together. We lodged two television sets in the antlers of a moose head, one control panel set on several stacks of books; flashing lights and screens peered from boxes and crates; speakers hung from every wall.

My sole job was to hold things in place while Peter secured them and quickly connected them electronically to something else. Soon wire cobwebbed the ceiling, and spare parts littered the floor. Peter finally carried the power cable onto the roof and connected it to the power lines. I waited in the basement and watched, feeling an odd sense of accomplishment. Suddenly sparks jumped from the moose antlers, lights went on, televisions brightened, and speakers cackled to life. A minute later,

Peter rushed down the steps and glanced around. "It's working!" he shouted.

"That's great," I said. "Now, what's it supposed to do?" The cellar now seemed like nothing more than a motley version of NASA's control center. The musty air of the cellar mixed with the sparky smell of ozone.

"You'll see," Peter said, and we continued working. That evening, we had take-out Chinese food as we sat in front of our control panels. I promised myself that I would never spend another day off like this again.

"So what will all this accomplish?" I asked through a mouthful of Bok Choy.

"We're listening for invaders," Peter answered. He was constantly monitoring the screens. Every now and then, he would shout an order to me regarding my panel; "Press that red button! No, not that one! The other one! The one in the corner! Yeh, yeh, good!" And then he would go back to his own controls, running his fingers over them like the world's fastest typist.

"By the way," I asked, "how do those video games figure in all this?" I pointed at the two full-sized arcade games, Pac-Man and Donkey Kong.

"I got them for you in case you got bored," he said.

After two more hours, I started putting quarters into the video games. Peter reassured me that he could get them out later. When my quarters ran out, I put my head on an old desk and dozed. Peter nudged me awake hours later. "You're going to have to take over," he whispered.

I rubbed my eyes. "What time is it?"

"Four A.M.," he said. "I need your help. It's an emergency. You'll have to take over."

I perked up. "What happened?" I asked.

"I'm hungry," he said. "I'm going to get some pizza from the 24-hour place down the block. You'll have to watch the screens while I'm gone. Here . . ." He handed me a switch that was hooked up to the controls.

"What's this?" I asked.

"It's hooked to a device that will convert any language to English. I made it for you while you slept."

"Made if for me?" I asked, still groggy. "Don't you need it, too?"

"I'm multilingual," he said. "Besides, you might not need it after all. The antenna box is on the fritz. I might have to fix it when I get back. By the way, do you like anchovies?"

I was left alone at the controls, not daring to touch any of the buttons. I kept on thinking about Peter, wondering what he was really about, why he was so smart, why he was living out this bizarre fantasy, and why in hell I was living it out with him, especially at four in the morning.

Suddenly I heard footsteps, but instead of Peter and the pizza, it was another tenant, Sophie Winkenwerber from the fourth floor. She had her laundry.

She glanced at the electrical equipment, then shrugged. I wasn't sure if Peter wanted to keep his operation a secret, but it was too late to do anything now. The antenna box was on the washing machine. Sophie moved it while she loaded the washer. On her way out, she stopped by the Donkey Kong game, put in a quarter, and started playing.

The washing machine was vibrating frantically, and the antenna box on its lid began sparking. I was about to move it when the speakers hissed to life. Surprised by the noise, I turned around.

There was the same hideous face on every screen, something between a Klingon from the film, "Star Trek," and the back side of a baboon. I glanced from one screen to the next, listening to the speakers, hearing a voice that sounded like a hippo with gastritis. I felt my Bok Choy coming up.

Sophie glanced up from her game. "I see Peter got hisself hooked up to the cable. He done it for just about everyone else in the building. It's about time he got it, too." She blew a bubble, popped it, and continued chewing.

"Yeah," I said, watching the screens, grateful that Sophie had come up with her own explanation to cover the reality, and wondering why "Petey" never hooked me up to cable!

"What's on? A sci-fi from Japan?" Sophie asked. "You'd think they'd have subtitles for what cable costs these days, even at this hour."

"Yeah," I said, "but you're not paying for cable, remember? 'Petey' hooked you up." Sophie ignored the sarcasm. I eyed the switch Peter made for me, impatiently waiting for Sophie to leave. When the game was over, she went up the stairs, and as soon as I heard the cellar door close above, I threw the switch.

The speakers cackled, and then I heard the voice in English: ". . . and we lost two ships, but we're in shape to attack."

The voice matched the mandible movement of the face, and then another voice came on, belonging to a face off-screen: "How many fleets will you have for your next attack?"

"Fourteen," the Klingon/baboon face answered. "But after we conquer Earth, we'll pick up six more on the trip back."

My neck hairs prickled when I heard "Earth." He couldn't mean here, could he? How would he know this planet's name? Or maybe, I hoped, there was another Earth somewhere. I desperately hoped Peter would come back soon!

"Do you plan to take any prisoners?" the off-screen alien asked.

"No reason to," the face answered, "except to fill our meat lockers. We're running desperately low on hamburger. Listen, I gotta sign off. It's time for my favorite soap opera."

"Later . . ."

Then all sound and images disappeared. I anxiously glanced at the big screen in front of me, then at the smaller ones in the antlers. Nothing!

I was suddenly afraid Peter wouldn't believe me. When I heard footsteps, I turned around. Peter was coming down the stairs with a large pizza box in his hands. "I hope you like mushrooms," he said. "The pizza place goofed big time!"

"Peter," I yelled. "They're coming! I heard them! I saw them! They're coming!" I gripped his sleeves, snaking the pizza box between us.

Peter glanced at me, his mouth open, but before he could say anything, a voice, but no face this time, came on, "Listen, buddy, I have some good Hookpeth for sale cheap!"

"Well, I don't know . . ." answered another voice.

"It'll make an interplanetary invasion more fun, keep you going for days, won't give you a hangover, and it can't be detected in a urine test. Furthermore . . ." Peter threw the translator switch, and the English was replaced by garbled rumblings.

"Holy cow!" Peter gasped, then, glancing at the antenna box on the shaking washing machine, he said, "You fixed it! How about that?"

"But you don't understand," I said. "They're coming here!"

"Who?" Peter asked.

I pointed at a blank screen. "Them!"

Peter's eyebrows rose so fast that his glasses snapped in half at the bridge. He twisted and caught them in his hands. "No kidding," he whispered, awed. "I could use some Hookpeth myself!" He blinked in astonishment, then shoved the pizza box at me. "Here. Take this. Eat it before it gets cold. We got work to do." He picked a lock on the Pac-Man machine, and quarters poured onto the floor as he started rearranging wires.

'How can you mess with that now?" I shouted. "We're being invaded!"

"Here! Take these quarters and keep the washing machine going," he ordered. "I don't want to lose contact with the invaders. And hand me a slice of pizza."

Eventually, Peter hooked the video game to his complicated communications system. Suddenly, the game appeared on all the sets. He quickly sat down at the keyboard console and began typing into the computer like a maniac.

"Now what's happening?" I asked.

"I'm blocking their ship-to-ship communications with the image of the video game," he said. "That way, they can't talk to each other."

"Ah," I said, feeling some relief. "And you're setting it to their wavelength with your computer?"

"No," he replied. "That's already taken care of. I'm typing in the directions in their language just in case any of them wants to play. That'll keep them distracted." He typed a little more, then threw a switch. "Done! Toss me your auto keys. I'm going to need your car." I held out the keys to the Bug and watched him dash up the stairs.

"When this is over with," I shouted after him, "I'd like to have a little word with you about cable!" But I don't think he heard me. The door slammed above. I felt reassured that Peter had everything under control. My body was a bundle of nerves. I put a few more quarters into the washing machine, then headed upstairs to my apartment for some coffee.

I was walking along the first floor to the stairs at the back of the hall when Mrs. Hedley stuck her head out of her apartment. She was in a tattered bathrobe and a frizzled nightgown, with dirty, wooly slippers on her feet. She stood all of four and a half feet tall. Without her wig, she was virtually bald. "You're up too," she said as I passed. "Everyone's up early this morning."

"Yes, Ma'am," I said, trying to walk on.

"Do you know what Peter told me?" Mrs. Hedley asked. I stopped and turned around. "He said that we're being invaded by people from outer space!" She emphasized the last two words with her finger in the air. "Now, what do you think of that?"

I thought it was crazy that Peter would breach the secrecy of such an important project with Mrs. Hedley. What if she really was from another planet? But after spending the night watching Peter work, I decided that he must know what he was going. "He's right," I finally confessed.

Mrs. Hedley squinted her eyes. "I see," she finally said. "You both must have gone to the same party."

"No, Mrs. Hedley, I'm serious."

She looked down at the floor and made a "Tch, tch, tch," sound.

"Look," I said, "if you don't believe me, let me show you."

"Oh, I believe you, dear," she said, patronizingly.

"No," I insisted, "I can show you. Really."

"You don't have to show me any people from outer space," Mrs. Hedley said. "It's a little early in the morning for them anyway, I'm sure."

"Just come and see," I said.

Mrs. Hedley sighed. "All right," she said.

Once in the cellar, I presented the entire setup to her. "It's a communications system," I said. "We were in contact with attacking starships."

"Starships," Mrs. Hedley said. She held a delicate porcelain cup and saucer, and she sipped some tea. "All I see is Pac-Man."

"We're using that to block their communications," I said. "That way, they will be in confusion until we can . . ." I gestured frantically. "Well, whatever Peter has in mind."

"You don't say," she remarked, her eyes sparkling.

"Yes," I said. "Do you believe me?"

Mrs. Hedley turned to me and smiled. "Sure, I believe you," she said. "You're a good tenant. You wouldn't lie. Hold this." She handed me her cup and saucer.

Before I knew what was happening, she reached into the robe and brought out what looked like a gun — a very strange gun, silver, with knobs and wires and tiny lights flashing.

Holding the gun with both hands, she took careful aim at the Pac-Man game and pulled the trigger. A succession of four blue sparks shot from the gun and hit the machine, blasting it into a pile of smoke, glass and wires.

My heart leaped into my throat. I glanced around. All the television screens were empty, and a flood of alien voices mixed with the sound of shorting wires. I turned angrily to Mrs. Hedley. "Do you know what you just did?" I shrieked.

She turned and pointed the gun at me. "I'm truly sorry it had to end this way," she said. "You're such a good tenant, but business is business."

"Mrs. Hedley, you wouldn't!" I gasped.

"I thought Peter was up to something," she said, gesturing with the gun. "I thought that if I made you think Peter told me about it, you would show me what was going on." She took careful aim at my chest.

"Drop it!" I heard from behind me.

Before I had a chance to look back, Mrs. Hedley grabbed me around the waist and twisted me in front of her. She was pretty strong for her age. I felt the gun at my ribs, and I heard her say, "Don't try anything or he gets it!"

There was Peter Monk, standing at the top of the cellar stairs. His hair was worse than normal, and his glasses were missing altogether. He had a laser gun in one hand and a gold badge in the other. "Intergalactic police!" he shouted. "You're under arrest!"

"YOU'LL HAVE TO SHOOT THROUGH HIM TO GET ME!" Mrs. Hedley shouted.

"I'll do what I have to do," Peter replied.

"Peter!" I screamed.

Peter gave me a sad glance. "Sorry," he said, "but business is business, you know." I felt my muscles tense. I closed my eyes. The teacup in my hands rattled in the saucer. I was aware of the sounds of humming machinery, and the sizzling, sparking, defunct video game. When Mrs. Hedley released her grip, I felt myself swoon with relief. My legs were jello, and it was all I could do to keep from passing out.

When I opened my eyes, I saw Peter putting handcuffs on Mrs. Hedley. They conversed in a language I never heard before. Then Peter directed her towards the stairs, and she started up by herself. I felt for a chair and sat down.

"Won't she get away?" I asked.

"If she tries," Peter said, "the cuffs will electrocute her."

"Who is she?" I asked.

"Didn't I tell you that she came from another planet?" Peter inquired. "She's an intergalactic spy, that's who she is."

I felt my stomach knot at his remark. "But what about the invasion?"

"A piece of cake!" Peter replied with enthusiasm. "I'm surprised I never thought of it before! I'll just have Mrs. Hedley send false information to the invaders. Let them think we have a plague here, and they'll panic and head back where they came from with their tails between their legs!"

Peter somehow paid off the equipment bills and ended up giving away most of the things he bought as he disassembled his "control room." He kept Donkey Kong, though, and was making scores in the zillions. When he finally got bored with the game, he turned it into a giant body massage and pizza-microwave.

As for me, Peter finally installed my cable. I made a habit of picking up lady hitchhikers, who weren't too impressed with my Bug until they saw how fast it went, and when they asked about the vibrating toothbrush on the dashboard, I'd tell them about this inventor friend of mine, and how one day we teamed up together and saved the world from an intergalactic invasion. It became one of my most successful lines.

BEAVER ATTACK

The evidence was right in front of her: a severely-gnawed kitchen table leg, just barely strong enough to support its share of the weight. Alice Vodwell set down the plate she was drying and bent over for a better view. "My God," she gasped, touching the tooth-marks with an arthritic finger.

She stood up and looked around. Past experience enabled her to spot the signs immediately: wood chips near the seldom-used cupboard beneath the sink. She opened the cupboard doors and reached into the damp storage area. This time she found three short, chewed-up lengths of what had once been a broomstick. "It's happening," she whispered to herself. "It's happening again!"

"Alice," Frank Vodwell called from upstairs. "How much longer will the roast be in the oven? The kids will be here in an hour, and the grandkids will be more than ready to eat."

Alice, her apron flapping, tromped into the hallway and stopped at the foot of the stairs. "Frank," she shouted, "come down here. We have to talk." She brushed a strand of gray hair from a wrinkled, chubby cheek, and felt something wet — a tear? — as she waited for her husband. She recalled the last time it happened, the last night of compounded horrors . . .

She stepped into the dining room, touching the tablecloth and looking at the table settings as her mind raced. "What is it, honey?" Frank asked as he came into the dining room. He wore dark brown pants and a white, long-sleeved shirt. Although his hair was black, compliments of Grecian Formula 16, his moustache retained enough gray to add distinction to his features. He smiled at his wife as he lit his pipe. "Dear, would you like . . ." His mouth dropped open. Alice, gazing into his face, held the broom handle pieces in her hand where he could see them.

"Frank," Alice said, "you said you quit the last time this happened." She put the pieces on the table next to a plate. "Now it's beginning again, isn't it?"

Frank quickly regained his composure. "Nonsense, Alice," he said, puffing on his pipe. "I'm cured, and you know it."

Alice pointed at the wooden pieces. "I know what I see," she said.

"Dry rot," Frank said, averting his gaze.

"And what about that?" Alice shouted, pointing into the kitchen. The gnawed table leg stood out like a sore thumb.

"A bad case of rats," Frank said without looking at it. "It's been that way for a long time. You just haven't noticed it."

Alice's face turned beet-red. She reached down her blouse and brought out a rusty skeleton key tied around her neck with a dirty length of twine. Holding the key between thumb and forefinger, she shook it close to his eyes. "I still have the key!" she said. "Tomorrow, I'm going to burn the suit!"

The pipe fell from Frank's lips. Tobacco and ash peppered the carpet. "No, Alice," he said. "You can't. Not the Beaver Suit! You promised!"

"And you promised not to give in to these . . . urges!" Alice gestured with her hands. "Frank, you need help. I'm not going to stand back and watch you become a victim to your sickness again!" She stuffed the key back down her blouse. "I'm calling Beavers Anonymous tomorrow."

"But . . . Susan and Jim . . ."

"We'll have dinner as planned," Alice said. "Just behave yourself. I don't want Susan and her husband driving home on chewed-up tires." She picked up the pieces of broomstick, gave Frank a look that meant she was dead-serious, and headed back to the kitchen.

Not taking his eyes off his wife, Frank picked up his pipe and backed towards the stairs. When he was sure that Alice was busy drying the silverware for the evening's meal, he quickly tiptoed upstairs. Slipping into the guestroom and closing the door behind him, he went to the closet. Just as Alice had warned, the closet door was locked tight, and she had the only key. But Alice didn't know that the hinges had been chewed off the doorframe.

Frank went to the double bed and reached beneath the mattress. He found the screwdriver that he hid the last time he thought about getting the suit. He shoved it between the doorframe and the door. Using the screwdriver as a lever, he pulled. The old wood groaned, but nothing gave way. Feeling a spasm of panic, he held his breath and pulled harder. The door screeched like an animal in a leghold trap. The hinges popped, sending the door crashing against the old oak dresser.

Frank fell backwards onto the floor, hitting his head on the foot of the bed. His ears rang and his vision blurred, but he pulled himself up and looked into the closet. There was nothing but dust, a few stray wooden hangers, and the Beaver Suit, seeming to stand in wait for its next mission. The suit hung from an ancient coat-hanger, empty, calling to Frank to be filled.

The fur was dark brown and gray, and the suit was tailor-made to Frank's body. The feet were complete with webbing and claws, and the humongous Beaver Tail could fan-cool a room on a hot afternoon. With shaking hands, Frank grasped the Beaver Head and examined it for damage from age. The whiskers were brittle, but the black nose still gleamed. The eyes were like two-way mirrors, with the outsides gloss black and the insides transparent. The teeth were like white, giant chisels, and the ears, by way of string controls, could wiggle.

Frank put the head on the bed and carefully brought the suit out of the closet. It felt heavy, as though it had gained weight in its old age. He held it against his chest and stroked it, coughing as dust floated off the suit.

"Frank!" Alice shouted, throwing open the bedroom door and standing in the doorway. "Don't you even think about it! You know what happens when you put the suit on."

Frank tightened his grip on the suit, which puffed dust like a broken vacuum cleaner bag. "No, Alice," he said. "I can't let you destroy it! I can't!" He began fumbling with the zipper.

"Stop!" Alice shouted. "Don't put it on! I'll let you keep it, if you'll just put it back! I'll even let you touch it once a month!"

"It won't work, Alice. You're just trying to trick me until you get a chance to burn it." Frank's eyes blazed with the urgency of a junkie grasping at his fix. With a shaking hand, he pulled the zipper halfway down until it stuck. "Damned Beaver Hair!" he groaned.

"Frank!" Alice pleaded. "Get this crazy idea out of your head! You're not a Beaver!" She grasped the suit, trying to get it out of his hands. Dust flew everywhere.

"Alice, you tore the armpit!" Frank shouted. "Alice, cut that out!" They fought and pulled at the suit.

* * * * *

Jim and Susan Andrews and their two children strolled up the walk to the front door. "Now remember," Susan said to Bobby and Tammy, "any trouble from you tonight and you go to bed early tomorrow night."

"And let's remember to leave early tonight," Jim said. "I still have to finish the Governor's speech for tomorrow."

"You should have had that speech finished last night," Susan said, gathering her children before her. She pulled a brush from her purse and began brushing Tammy's hair.

"Ow!" Tammy cried.

"Quiet," Susan said. "You'd better shape up, Jim. If you cause one more problem for the Governor, you may end up pounding the sidewalk for another job."

Jim raised an eyebrow as he ran a comb through his dark-blond hair. "Just because I got one of his speeches mixed up with your letter to Aunt Mildred doesn't mean I'm doomed." He smiled and straightened his tie. "Besides, he caught on when he got to the part about Mrs. Filbert's hysterectomy, and from there, he winged it pretty well."

Susan went over Bobby's hair with the brush, then did her own. "Well, we can leave early tonight, but be sure to act nice to my folks. They helped us out a few times, remember?"

"Okay, okay," Jim said, adjusting his jacket. "But your father sure is strange sometimes."

He raised a fist to knock on the door, but before he placed the first knock, the door flew open wide. Jim's jaw dropped open. Standing before him was the biggest Beaver he ever saw! For that matter, he had only seen beavers in nature magazines, and he never imagined that they could grow so big, let alone stand on two legs. He screamed and jumped behind his wife and children.

The Beaver, standing six feet tall, was watching the hallway stairs when he opened the door. He turned around when Jim screamed, knocking a lamp off an end table with his tail. A shout came from the top of the stairs, and the Beaver looked back again. Alice Vodwell was charging down the steps, taking them two at a time on shaky legs. The Beaver let out a squawk and shoved past Jim and his family. He dashed into the street, leaping out of the way of a car.

"Stop him!" Alice shouted, dashing out the door.

"Good Lord!" Jim exclaimed, holding Bobby against his body.

"Jim!" Susan shouted.

"What?"

"Aren't you going to help Mother?"

Jim watched Alice and the Beaver disappear around a house. "If your mother wants to chase wild animals in the night, that's her business. I'm staying out of it."

"Did the Beaver eat our dinner?" Tammy asked over the noise of Bobby's giggling.

"No!" Susan shouted. "Jim, you . . . "

"Will Gramma cook the Beaver if she catches it?" Tammy asked.

"Quiet!" Susan yelled, slapping her hand against her own thigh. "Jim, do something!"

"Don't worry," Jim said, putting Bobby down and pointing. "Your mother's coming back now."

Susan turned and saw Alice running back to the house. "Jim what's going on?   Motherrr. . ." Alice dashed past them and ran into the house. "Mother!" Susan shouted, following her in with the children. Jim straightened his tie and followed his wife.

Alice, her hair a gray, wiry mess, was on the phone. "It's an emergency," she panted. "Yes, I need help."

Jim stepped forward and raised an eyebrow. "Who are you talking to?" he asked.

"Mother," Susan asked, "what's going on?"

"Hush!" Alice said. She focused on her telephone conversation. "Yes, this is Alice Vodwell at 195 Brewer. My maiden name?"

"Who's she calling?" Jim asked Susan.

Alice listened for a minute, then shook her head. "They put me on hold!" she told Susan. "Can you believe that?"

"Who put you on hold?"

"Mother," Susan said. "What is happening?"

Alice, her eyes watery, looked away. "Your father's gone crazy."

"Crazy?" Susan gasped.

Alice nodded. "He's wearing the Beaver suit!"

Susan glanced at the open front door, then at her mother. "That was Dad?"

Jim stared at Susan. "Your father's a Beaver?"

"Oh, God," Susan gulped.

"Why didn't you stop him?" Jim demanded. "That's all I need is to have the Governor find out that my father-in-law is a Beaver!"

Alice held the receiver to her ear with both hands. "Wait, I think I got through! Hello. . ."

"Are you calling the police?" Jim asked.

"Yes," Alice said. "Hello, I'm . . ."

"No!" Jim shouted. He reached at the phone and pressed the receiver button. "Don't tell the police anything! It would get to the press! I'll lose my job!"

Alice turned on him, her face full of rage. "You idiot!" she yelled, slamming the receiver on the cradle and his finger. "You don't know Frank the way I know him! Once he has the Beaver suit on, it's almost impossible to stop him! It's a sickness with him, an addiction!"

"But I never knew . . ." Susan whispered.

Jim sucked his throbbing finger, then glanced at Alice. "That's the most ridiculous thing I ever heard!" he said. He turned towards his wife. "Susan, if your father does something to embarrass me, I'll . . ."

"You'll what?" Susan snarled, gritting her teeth.

"Quiet! The both of you!" Alice shouted. "Can't you understand? It's not Frank's fault he's this way." Alice removed her apron and set it over a chair. "He's the victim of military medical experiments."

"Mother," Susan said, "what are you talking about?"

Alice glanced at a framed photograph of Frank wearing his youth, along with an army private's uniform. "He suffered shell shock during the war," she said, taking the photo from the mantel. "Army medicine was just beginning experiments on the practical application of Beaver Therapy. They thought a Beaver Suit might help Frank get well. Of course it worked, but they didn't know when to stop the therapy. Soon, Frank was hooked . . ."

Alice coughed into her fist and swallowed before she went on. "He never mentioned it when we got married, but deep down inside I knew something was wrong. At first I couldn't admit it to myself, but after the neighbors' firewood turned to wood chips, and one of our trees, gnawed at the roots, fell onto our house, it was obvious that Frank had a serious problem."

Susan dabbed at a tear with Bobby's sweater. Jim adjusted his tie.

Alice blew her nose and went on. "We tried marriage counseling, group therapy and Beavers Anonymous, but nothing worked. Then Frank put on the Beaver Suit, and all hell broke loose. Once he puts on that suit . . ." Alice stopped talking. Now, she only stared into space, watching far-off events of another time in her life.

"Mother, are you okay?" Susan whispered.

Alice glanced at her daughter, then blinked and shook her head. "We're wasting time," she said. "I think Frank headed west, away from town. Susan, I'll need you to help get some things out of the attic." She faced her son-in-law. "Jim, you take the kids in the car and try to track Frank down."

"Now, wait a minute!" Jim said, shaking his head. "Don't get me involved in all this!"

"Jim!" Susan shouted.

"Susan, I'm not your father's caretaker."

Alice glanced at Jim, knitting her eyebrows together. "I don't know why you married this Bozo, Susan."

"Jim," Susan said, "Daddy helped you finish college. He paid the down payment on our house. How can you talk this way now?"

"Susan . . ." Jim began.

"Let him go," Alice said. "We can't make Jim help if he doesn't want to. The police can take care of it." She put down Frank's army picture and picked up the phone.

"Wait!" Jim said. Alice looked at him, and he looked back. "This is blackmail."

Alice didn't answer his remark, but said, "You'll look for him then."

"Yes, I'll look," Jim huffed.

Alice smiled. "Good. And remember, if you see him, don't do a thing. Just call here and wait for us."

Jim ran his fingers through his hair and shook his head. "I could probably wrestle him to the ground. He's not very young, you know."

"Well, you're not very strong for a young man, you know." Alice said.

Jim's cheeks puffed out, then he sighed. "C'mon, kids," he said, taking their hands and heading for the door.

"That Beaver sure smelled like mothballs," Tammy told Bobby. Then she asked her father, "Do we still get dessert if we don't eat dinner?"

"Oh, shut up," Jim mumbled, and they headed for the car.

Susan shook her head as she closed the front door. "Mom, I never knew . . ."

Alice hugged her daughter. "Susie, just because he's a Beaver doesn't mean he's no longer your father." She let Susan go and turned away. "The last time this happened we tried every trick but one. Maybe tonight's the night for that last trick, and with the element of surprise on our side, maybe we'll end this thing once and for all."

"Mom?" Susan said, subdued, "what if it doesn't work?"

"I don't know," Alice said. "I just don't know." She turned around. "Come with me to the attic. I'll need your help." They headed upstairs together, neither one sure of what the outcome of the evening would be.

*   *   *   *   *

"Now, just what did you say, young man?" the transient asked. He was an old man, with a Santa Claus beard, a toothless smile, and a railroad cap perched on a shaggy, gray head.

Jim looked at the other five transients standing under the sharp glare of the streetlight, then back at the old man again. He was tempted to roll up the car window and drive on. "I wanted to know if you saw a . . . a very large Beaver recently."

"Yeah, but didn't you say this was a six-foot-high Beaver?" the old man asked. He looked like he was about to laugh.

"Thazz what I heard," Bessie, a short, stout bag lady behind him said. "He sez . . . He sez, A Beaver six-foot tall!"

Jim felt his cheeks flush.

A skinny man in dirty overalls and tennis shoes but no shirt or socks stepped forward. "Did this Beaver wear a red tie and patent leather shoes?"

"What?" Jim sputtered. "No! Of course not!"

"Oh," the man replied. "I guess that musta been another six-foot tall Beaver!" The group of transients burst out laughing.

"Look," Jim shouted. "You're being ridiculous!"

Jessie stroked his beard as he turned to the skinny man. "Now, see here, Chubby! This gentleman here says that you're being ridiculous!" They all laughed again. "Now, cut it out afore I slap you up aside o' the head!"

Feeling his cheeks burning, Jim reached for the ignition. Tammy, his daughter, shoved herself past his shoulder and stuck her head out the driver's window. "The Beaver is my grandpa!" she shouted. "Don't laugh at him!"

The laugher died down, and the transients contemplated her words. A man in blue jeans and tattered t-shirt stepped forward. "Just what is she talking about, Mister?"

Jim looked up at him. "My father-in-law is running around, dressed up in a Beaver Suit."

"Well that explains everything," the man said. "You'll find your Beaver down on McKay Street." The other transients looked at him.

"You saw him?" Jim asked.

"Yeah, about ten minutes ago."

"So why didn't you say anything when I first asked?"

The man scratched his belly. "If you saw a giant Beaver running around, would you brag about it?"

"I guess not," Jim said. "Thanks for the information." He started the car, and they drove on. Jim looked in his rearview mirror to make sure that Tammy and Bobby were all right, then turned down McKay Street.

It had turned out to be a most miserable night. His wife, Susan, was at the house with her mother, Alice Vodwell, while her father, Frank Vodwell, was roaming the streets dressed in a realistic Beaver outfit. Whatever was wrong with Jim's father-in-law had something to do with experiments during his stay in the army. Regardless of the reasons, this was no mere Halloween party trick. Frank was going through something, and probably all but believed that he was a real Beaver. And now, Jim Andrews had to find him!

As they drove along McKay Street, Jim spotted the first Beaver Sign: chew marks on the side of an oak. "Keep your eyes open!" he told the kids. Tammy gripped her pony tails with excitement, and Bobby picked his nose.

"Oh, if any of this gets to the Press," Jim muttered, "I'm through!" As a speech writer for the Governor, his work had lately been questioned, especially after the Governor's last speech, when Jim somehow got the pages of the speech mixed up with Susan's letter to Aunt Mildred, and the Governor didn't catch on until he got to the part about Aunt Mildred's hysterectomy.

They drove on, spotting a chewed-up picket fence, a pile of scattered, gnawed-up firewood, and a crudely dammed-up fishpond in someone's suburban lawn. At one house, a carport had toppled onto a car. The support beams had been gnawed in half, and the owner, confused and furious, was stomping around his damaged vehicle.

"Daddy!" Tammy shouted, pointing. "The Beaver! The Beaver!" Jim stopped the car and looked. The Beaver appeared from the shadows between two houses, his great tail pounding the ground as he ran. He was a formidable sight, looking realistic as he charged across the street just in front of them. They heard a shotgun blast, and the Beaver leaped and stumbled on, holding his rump. A man with a shotgun ran out of the shadows, screaming and shaking a fist at the Beaver. He stopped under a streetlight and fired again, but the Beaver had just turned around the corner of another house.

Jim hit his high beams and floored the gas pedal. The car leaped forward as he turned off the road, bumped over the sidewalk and drove across somebody's front lawn and between two houses. He could see the Beaver just ahead, and slowed down to keep some distance between them. The car squeaked and groaned as Jim's shocks crunched in protest. Jim had never driven through rose beds before, and he prayed that nobody could read his license plate. Charging through another backyard, he inadvertently disassembled a swing set with a loud crash and grazed the side of an above-ground swimming pool, effectively emptying it of its water. Jim gritted his teeth but kept going, thinking of how close he was to losing his job, and how, just because his sister was married to the Governor, he wouldn't be forgiven forever.

He bounced through a ditch onto another road, losing his mufflers and hearing a sickening crunch in the back. Sweat froze on his body as he suddenly remembered that the kids were back there. "Bobby!" he screamed. "Tammy!"

"What?" Tammy shouted back.

"Are you guys okay?"

"Yeah, let's do that again!" Tammy giggled.

Jim sighed. "How's Bobby?"

"He's okay, but he needs new pants."

"New pants?"

"And socks," Tammy added. "And a towel to dry the seat."

Bobby and Tammy giggled together. Jim groaned, slowing the car and keeping his eyes on the Beaver, who still gripped his rump. He switched off the headlights, hoping that the Beaver would find a place to stop so he could call his wife and mother-in-law and report that he'd found him. He had no idea what Alice had in mind, but he hoped and prayed that it would work.

*   *   *   *   *

"They found Daddy!" Susan announced.

"Where?" Alice asked, carrying a large, dusty cardboard box into the kitchen.

Susan talked on the telephone again, nodding and glancing at her mother. "He's at the supermarket near the highway. He says Daddy's tired out and resting behind the store. It sounds like he's been very busy."

"Then we'd better make our move!" Alice said. "Tell Jim to stay put. Tell him not to do a thing until we get there!" She set the box down on the kitchen table. The gnawed leg finally snapped, and the table and box went crashing to the floor. "Oh, dear!" Alice said, gathering her skirt together as she knelt to pick up the box. "Sometimes your father is so much trouble I wonder why I never got a divorce!"

"Jim wants to know why he has to stay put." Susan said, covering the mouthpiece. "He thinks he can catch Daddy."

Alice shook her head. "Jim's more useful when he does nothing at all."

"Motherrr . . . "Susan hissed. "At least he found Daddy!"

"Is there anything else?" Alice asked.

"Wait," Susan said, then talked to Jim again. "Yes, dry clothes for Billy."

"I'll get something for him," Alice said as she hauled the bulky box onto the kitchen counter. "Just tell Jim to stay put until we get there."

"I did."

"Tell him again," Alice said as she left the kitchen.

Susan put the phone to her ear. "Take care, and don't do anything until we get there. And don't forget, I love you, and Mom loves you too."

"That's debatable," Alice called from the living room. Susan hung up the phone and folded her arms. She paced the kitchen, then glanced at the box on the table. She ran her finger over the layer of dust, making a design, then noticed the faded emblem of the Beaver standing next to a man with a butterfly net. The initials, B.A. were beneath the picture, and below that, in parentheses, the words, "Beavers Anonymous."

"Mother," Susan whispered as Alice reappeared with a gallon can of gasoline. "Just what it this anyway?"

"This," Alice began, cutting the strings around the box with a paring knife, "is the only way we have of stopping your father by ourselves before we have to call in the SWAT team." She lifted the lid, and Susan glanced inside.

"Mother, you're kidding, aren't you?"

"Drastic times require drastic measures."

"But this . . ." Susan gestured at the box. "If the police catch Daddy, he'll make the front page. If they catch you with this, we'll all be talking to Oprah Winfrey!"

"These are serious times," Alice said. "The last time your father put on the Beaver Suit, I had to dig a ten-foot-deep hole in the backyard to trap him. The neighbors helped get him out and tie him up. I know he won't fall for any Beaver Trap this time. This is our only hope."

"What's this?" Susan asked, holding an old pump-spray bottle.

Alice snatched it out of her hands and put it back in the box. "Don't touch things if you don't know where they came from!"

"Motherrr . . ."

"Now pick up that gas can and follow me," Alice said, carrying the box to the front door. "We've got a Beaver to catch."

* * * * *

"Ohhhh . . . " Frank moaned. The buckshot in his buttocks felt like a thousand bee stings. "Ohhhh . . . " he repeated. His body was drenched in sweat, his muscles ached, and his head felt like a drum in a band that had just finished playing a marathon of John Phillip Sousa songs. He considered the pain in his chest, wondering if it was a heart attack getting ready to happen. This wasn't as much fun as it was in his youth.

But the Beaver Suite gave him the power of anonymity, a hiding place in his own body, the way a turtle's shell was its own home. In the army, the Beaver Suite was a crazy replacement for his uniform, and allowed him to break away from the regimentation of his fellow soldiers. The Beavers Suit allowed him to play the animal, to let his imagination go wild. And — he once thought in the army — people shoot people, not Beavers. Tonight he discovered that he was wrong.

"Oh Lord . . ." Frank moaned, leaning against a dumpster and studying his tattered, webbed feet. The Suit was falling apart! The tail was no longer straight and powerful, but bent, tattered and worn. His white chisel teeth were chipped and broken, and his mechanical jaw squeaked and sometimes stuck. The suit was ripping everywhere, not from the running and escaping but simply from old age. Oh, the night was miserable!

And to top it all off, there was that Bozo in the car who chased him for several blocks. Frank thought he'd never lose him. His stomach growled, and he thought about the dinner his family was to have, and he wondered if they ate without him. He couldn't blame them if they did. He felt as though he were the most childish person in the world.

He thought about his daughter and his son-in-law. Then he thought about his grandchildren, and how he hoped they didn't inherit too many genes from Jim. He thought about all the violence on television, and all the stupid sitcoms, and soap operas, and commercials, and talk shows . . . and even that speech the Governor gave about the deficit, more federal spending cuts, higher crime rates, and hysterectomies. With so many problems like that in the world, small wonder he wanted to hide inside a Beaver Suit!

"Ohhhhh . . ." he moaned.

"Ahhhh . . ." somebody answered. He glanced up, turned to the next dumpster, and saw the Skunk. With large bosoms, flashy whiskers, and an exotic black-and-white tail, she was the most attractive Skunk he had ever seen. The oddity of her five-foot-seven height escaped him on a busy night like this.

Frank rubbed his glass-covered eye holes and looked again. The Skunk kept her hands behind her back, but she wiggled her rump and curled her tail. He waved. She winked. He tried to move his tail, but the controlling cables were broken. But perhaps she would overlook his infirmities. He cautiously approached and sniffed. She seductively wiggled her whiskers.

Something wanting, deep inside his soul, made his sore heart beat faster. He stepped closer, and she tilted her head. He blinked; she snickered; he snacked. Then he reached out to touch her glistening fur. He couldn't feel anything through his Beaver Gloves, but he believed that he could live with this Skunk forever. Then he thought about his wife, Alice, back at the reality of his home. He wondered how upset she would be if she found out that he had run off with a Skunk.

In that moment, when Frank, lost in the dizziness of his Beaver Suit, was contemplating interspecies relationship possibilities, Alice, in her Skunk Suit, brought the spray bottle from behind her back and began spraying him.

"What the . . ."

"Frank, you asked for this!" Alice shouted.

"Hey! What's going on?" Frank backed away. "Hey, you're not a real Skunk! Alice, is that you in there? Alice, I wasn't going to run away with any skunk, honest!"

"Frank, you're gonna hate me for this, but I'm doing this for your own good!"

"What are you saying?" Frank demanded. "What are you talking about, Alice?" And then he noticed the horrible odor. "Good Lord!" Frank gasped, still unaware of the spray bottle in Alice's paw. "What's that terrible stink?"

"Essence of Skunk," Alice said.

"Gaaah!" Frank screamed, yanking off the Beaver Head and tossing it aside. The stench enveloped him, burning his nostrils and making his eyes water. He fell onto the ground and rolled back and forth, pulling off the gloves, kicking off the webbed feet, and frantically fumbling at the rusty zipper.

Alice stood back and watched, removing the Skunk Head for a better view. When Frank had the Suit off and backed away, she gave the signal. Susan appeared from the shadows, and before Frank had a chance to react, she doused the Beaver Suit with gasoline. Alice struck a wooden match on the dumpster, and as Frank watched, horrified, she tossed the match. The Suit burst into flame in one air-consuming whoosh, and Frank's jaw dropped open.

"My Suit!" Frank gasped, standing.

"We had to do it, Frank," Alice said.

Frank, shivering in his white boxer shorts, t-shirt, and socks, stepped towards the flames. "My Suit . . ." Susan took his arm and tried to lead him away. "My Suit . . ."

"It's time to go home, Frank," Alice said as Jim drove up and stepped out. The car sounded like a diesel generator without its mufflers, and the paint was scratched and scraped. Jim straightened his tie and opened the door as Alice and Susan guided Frank into the back seat. Tammy and Bobby hugged their grandfather as he sat beside them. The ashen pile of old cloth and burning hairs crackled and gave off a nasty odor as the flames died down.

"My Suit . . . " Frank said as they drove off.

A quiet breeze blew smoke and ashes toward the night sky. At the farthest dumpster, the lid opened a crack. Four eyes peered cautiously at the smoldering pile. "There's a lesson to be learned here, Ed."

"Yeah, Barney."

"It just goes to show you where wild behavior will get you."

"Totally sad. It looks like the old boy got carried away." The dumpster lid was pushed open with a clang, and two large Beaver Heads peered over the side. "You wanna do a few more trees, before we go home, Barney?"

"No can do," Barney said. "My wife thinks I'm bowling tonight. I gotta be home early, you know."

"Yeah, you're right," Ed said. "I'm feeling a little tired tonight myself." The two Beavers climbed carefully out of the dumpster, glanced around, and dashed into the shadows, their massive Beaver Tail's thumping the ground and they ran.

GRANDFATHER CARP

The slag from the old Pennsylvania coal mines dammed up the creek, creating the deep, dark lake. Tall grasses, blackberries and maple trees were reclaiming most of the black moonscape, but the air still stank of slate, coal dust, and tar. Larry Johnson, CPA, clumsily put a hook and two lead sinkers onto the end of his fishing line while eyeing the black water of the lake.

Larry Johnson, CPA, was the sort of man Rod Serling might have referred to at the beginning of every episode of "The Twilight Zone," an ordinary man living an ordinary life in which nothing exciting ever happened. One day, walking his daschund, "Dependent," down a dirt road and along a well-worn path through the woods, he found the small lake. It was small as lakes go, and deserted, but for a solitary fisherman in waders who already hooked four rainbow trout that morning. It was from the fisherman that he heard the story of Grandfather Carp, a fish so large he had to be older than the lake itself.

Larry Johnson, CPA, wasn't a fisherman by any stretch of the imagination, but he was a dreamer. He could see Grandfather Carp stuffed and mounted over his fireplace mantle, next to the bowling trophy he won ten years ago. There was a general store/post office/hardware store at the beginning of the road, so Larry and Dependent walked the two miles back to it. There, Larry bought the largest fishing pole he could find.

"It'll break if you hook Grandfather Carp," Mrs. Weatherbee, the proprietor, said, after Larry mentioned his plans. "But take this. Grandfather Carp will come for you." She handed him a dog whistle wrapped in plastic.

"You're crazy," Larry said, but bought it anyway. "If this fishing rod isn't strong enough, what should I use?"

"A harpoon," Mrs. Weatherbee said, adjusting her prince-nez glasses and tending to the next customer.

The fisherman was gone when Larry got back to the lake. Larry prepared his rod and waded waist-deep into the water. He cast his line out, then pulled the dog whistle from his pocket, blowing a silent note. Dependent, resting on the grassy shore, raised his head, but nothing else happened. Larry blew again.

The water churned less than fifty feet from shore. With the fishing rod gripped in one trembling hand, Larry blew a third time. "Here we go . . ." he said, just as a large fish head broke from the water. Grandfather Carp leaped, twisting in the air, snapping his massive jaws shut, rising again, with two legs kicking frantically from his mouth as he fell back into the dark, churning water. Larry Johnson, CPA, was gone.

Dependent watched for another minute, then laid his head back on his paws. The dog whistle had been irritating, and he was grateful that it was now silent. He dozed, basking in the early afternoon sun.

THE CIVIL WAR
ROCKS
INSECTS
BOTTLE CAPS
FLORIDA
TEE-SHIRT
30 EACH
LIFE
POLY'S
AU-H2O
HOME
SWEET
HOME
1 2 3 4 5 6
7 8 9 10 11 12 13
14 15 16 17 18 19 20
21 22 23 24 25 26 27
28 29 30 31
PILL
BOTTL
50 B
MAGAZINE
200 EA
POWER
WORDS
200
EACH
READ
DIG
100
RADIO
PARTS
10 CASES
100 DIALS
100 KNOBS
GOOD
STUFF SAVE

LISTING

It's the Canaga Curse, you know. I talked to my mother about it the other day. Like me, she collects house fans, hotel towels, restaurant ashtrays, National Geographics, unmatched socks (we each have a large, cardboard box of them), placemats from fast food places, old newspapers, Reader's Digest, radios we plan to fix someday, postcards, souvenirs from every state, t-shirts with messages on them, TV Guides . . . We categorize our things, listing them, my mother in her old mobile home, me in my crowded apartment.

Listing is our fate. Our homes are full to overflowing. We have paths through out rooms, paths like the Colorado River cutting through the Grand Canyon, with canyon walls of books and old magazines and cardboard boxes. The Canaga Curse.

One day Grandma Canaga fell and broke her hip in her house. If she had broken her hip on the way to the grocery, or hitchhiking to Los Angeles, or even crossing an arctic glacier, she would have had a much better chance of survival. As it was, she starved to death. She didn't have the strength to drag her way along the path through the yellowed newspapers, dusty boxes and stacks of photo albums to the telephone. The postman later reported looking through the windows, but he couldn't see beyond the stacks and boxes.

Of course, Mom and I inherited the Canaga Curse long before Grandma died, but when we inherited her boxes, stacks and brown paper bags as well, we were both overwhelmed. It was confusing at first, but after we divided Grandma's things between us, made our lists, and put everything in its proper stack or pile, things pretty much got back to normal.

I was discussing all this with my mother by phone the other day, just hours before fire destroyed her mobile home and everything inside it. The loss of all those precious things would surely have killed Mother, had not the fire gotten to her first. She wanted to be cremated anyway, and she would have appreciated the romantic touch of taking her things with her.

Naturally I became despondent about losing my grandmother and mother in the same month. I wandered the paths through my apartment for weeks on end, touching my stacks and revising my lists. My friends sent their condolences in cards and letters, and I put them all safely away in a cardboard box. I tried categorizing my friends, listing them, but they couldn't be stacked, boxed or stored.

When the police came, I had lost sixty pounds. I'd been meaning to go on a diet for years. After a few months at the hospital, I got a new apartment. My friends still worry about me, since most of my stuff was taken to the dump by the health department during my absence. But there's nothing to worry about. I collect stamps and coins now. And antiques. And books. And minerals. And postcards.

It's the Canaga Curse, you know.

SCHULTZ '97

CALLING

The Willamette Valley with her trees and hills and houses and people and Rachel and the baby we were going to have and the Willamette River running through it all called to me like a distant white bird, and after three months I answered the call. I came. In Eugene, Oregon, Rachel told me once, the rains last ten months out of the year like a special season.

They were gentle rains, sacred rains that Eugenians walk and bicycle through with no more than a passing thought as autumn leaves turn color and the smelled of the coming winter permeate the air with woodstove smoke, decaying vegetable gardens, damp leaves, mud and spicy kitchen smells. I breathed deep, feeling the cold air inflate my lungs and reach through my veins. I'd just hitched a ride from the Southern Oregon border, the fifth ride since Southern California two days ago, where the peach harvesting left me with a wad of money in my pocket. I could've taken a Trailways up Highway 101 along the coast to Florence then headed inland, but I had to answer the call on my own terms.

The truck driver dropped me off near the Ferry Street Bridge and drove off in a gust of diesel while I walked over the Willamette River to Skinner's Butts in the Oregon autumn night. What with the misty rain and the closed storefronts and the chimneys smoking and the houselights watching, I felt lonely and enchanted. I walked along the bicycle trail near the river, listening to the distant murmurs of highway traffic and the heartbeat rumble of an unseen freight train. Stopping under a street lamp I held my wet face up to see the raindrops coming down at me like a gift of scattered gleaming stars.

Fifteen minutes later I came to the Millhouse Pub, a large refurbished building on the river that vibrated with jazz and smell of beer and greasy fried potato skins, and I stepped through the door, stopped and shook some of the wetness off. The saxophone plowed its magic through smoky air while men and women sat at tables sharing pitchers of beer. Billiard balls clicked and the dart board announced the next point with a thock as the music hummed the room in saintly rhythms.

I took an empty booth in back and ordered a large bottle of Tooth Sheath Ale and a basket of fried mushrooms with a bowl of vinegar. I restlessly ate a few as I watched the stage. Rachel was up there under the red lights, perched forward on the stool as though she might topple over but still defied gravity. Her long black hair cascaded over her shoulders and forehead, hiding her face. Her feet danced on the stool leg brace to the rhythm as she held her microphone to her lips and sang wordless sounds, "...do-wop-de-diddy-do-do-unhuh-do..." a clear voice in tandem with the ensembles of drums, sax, bass and piano, rumbling static and prophetic through the dark room.

When they finished their set, I ordered another Tooth Sheath and a Hamm's beer. Rachel dismounted, leaving her mike on the stool. She was tall and thin, with small breasts beneath a folksy silk blouse and an intricate blue Tibetan vest. A cotton Andes skirt covered her legs, and she wore Birkenstocks on her bare feet. Large brown eyes gazed at me from behind round wire-rimmed glasses. Her small mouth and upturned nose gave her a little girl look.

She fingered her hair back from her face before she sat next to me. Her body smelled of sweat and rainwater and frankincense. She smiled, her arms went around me and mine around her. We kissed long, softly, gentle, and then we looked at each other, refamiliarizing ourselves. "Howdy, Sailor Man," she said. "Metta."

"Namaste," I answered, adding "Jazz Girl." I held her hands in mine. Only her hands revealed she was in her mid-thirties. "You sound great tonight.'"

"Why didn't you tell me you were coming back?" she asked, a smile dimpling her cheeks. "I almost lost it on stage when I saw you sitting here."

"I sent a postcard a week ago. A picture of the California coast. I even wrote a haiku on the side," I recited it from memory.

Long slow road through life.
Mountain spirits whisper cloud.
Passing sleepy towns.

"Didn't you get it?" I asked kissing her fingers. "So what's going on?"

A shadowy dark bird crossed her face. I felt winter brush my back. Wrinkles appeared around her eyes and she looked away. Her hand tightened on mine as shoulders trembled. "The baby's gone. I wrote you a letter last week. I guess you didn't get it."

I couldn't find an answer; it wasn't in my repertoire. It was only three months ago I began adjusting to the idea of being a father. I pulled her closer, rested my hand on her belly as though my touch could heal whatever was wrong. "Oh, Rachel, I'm so sorry."

"Just be with me," she said.

I rocked her against me wondering if it would have been a boy or a girl. She told me how it happened while she was shopping at the Kiva grocery story. She picked up a bag of brown rice and a bunch of celery when the woman behind her began pointing and shouting in Spanish. Blood dripped on the linoleum and she suddenly felt sick and terribly ashamed. I told her I wished I was there, but that's not what I felt.

She played one more set, then at two a.m. as she helped the band pack up, I got her knapsack and alpaca sweater. In the rain we walked past the University of Oregon where "Animal House" was filmed in the '70's - we'd seen it a dozen times - I reminded her of the first film we'd seen together at the Bijou Theater; "Choose Me," with Keith Carradine and Rae Dawn Chong.

I was amazed at my own weariness as we walked through dark streets, shiny and slick with rainwater like black obsidian. I held Rachel's hand as she talked about meeting Dizzy Gillespie once before he died, how his cheeks puffed out like a bullfrog's throat would when he played his horn.

Her apartment was sleeping dog warm when we got there. She put on a Charlie Parker C.D. Minutes later we were in her tub, touching and kissing and soaking in the steamy light of dozens of candles, holding long-stemmed wine glasses, and eating crackers and cheese from a stool by the tub. "Remember the first time we did this?" she asked.

"You put on Ravel's 'Bolero' and I knocked the whole plate of crackers into the water."

"And then you had to help me out of the tub because I got a cramp in my leg!" she laughed and I was glad she remembered. I rubbed my nose in her wet hair, smelling shampoo and the essence of her being.

Later we made love, breaking a sweat against every tomorrow to come, and later when it was over we touched each other, our fingers sliding along wet skin. "Are you sorry?" she asked. "Are you sorry I lost the baby?"

"I don't know," I replied, cupping her breast. The aureoles were like dark wild strawberries. "How can you feel sorry about something you can't control?"

"I was afraid you wouldn't come back this time."

"But I did," I said. "How do you feel about . . . what happened?" I couldn't say it just then. It didn't feel right.

"Empty," she murmured. Then she held me tight against something so ominous in the darkness I did not yet see. I held her close. We were slick as San Francisco seals smelling like the sea. Tears poured from my eyes, salty tears I wouldn't let her see. When Rachel was finally asleep I carefully untangled myself, silently put my clothes on and slipped out.

I walked the streets of Eugene, putting my collar up against the chill and rain and neon lights of stores that would be opening in a few hours. I was weighed down by weariness and sorrow, but something inside needed to keep moving. I walked through alleys, stomped through puddles. Somewhere wind chimes tinkled thoughtfully.

I found myself back at the river where I squatted on the muddy bank. The Willamette nodded at me like an old friend passing by, and the roaring waters drowned out my feelings. My clothes were saturated. Not even a Eugenian would be here at this hour, I realized. I sighed, then stood. The river pulled at me, called to me with a desperate urgency as I reached into my pocket and felt the wad of bills. Rachel knew me better than I knew myself. I had to make a decision soon, and this time I did not feel up to it.

PLANTING

As the crummy barreled along the precariously narrow logging road through the Oregon Cascade Range like a bobcat with stinging nettles up its ass, meandering through the steep tree stump and blackberry vine landscapes, nobody was aware that Old Bill Mulligan, leaning against the back heater, was deader than a Willamette River rock. For all we knew, Old Bill could've passed into his next Karmic life any time during the three hour drive from Eugene.

We arrived at seven a.m. near the clearcut timber line on the eastern slope, and though Old Bill was pretty ripe by the time we stopped, we chalked it up to his usual personal hygiene habits and assumed he was asleep. We left him behind to snooze as we filed out into the icy drizzle, one by one, picked up our tree packs with fifty pounds of ten-inch-long Douglas firs and started our planting lines, swinging hoedads over our heads into the mud, putting in a tree and moving on.

We worked ten feet apart, up and down from each other along the mountain side, our lines of trees parallel to each other as our hoedads cut arcs over our heads and packs became lighter, one tree at a time. By the end of the morning we waded up the muddy slope with empty packs and big appetites.

At lunch break we noticed Old Bill wasn't eating, and he looked a little more scraggly than usual. "Goddam, Bill," Crooked River Pete Buchannon said, puffing on a joint between bites of his peanut butter and bologna on rye. "You can't play possum all day, Zeb'll catch on!"

Luke Hargreaves, sitting next to him, gave him a shove, and Old Bill toppled over like a sack of rutabagas. The stench hit us good, like cabbage fermenting into sauerkraut. Appetites evaporated like rubbing alcohol on a California tan as we realized why he'd been so quiet all morning, but Luke still checked for a pulse, then held his coke mirror beneath Bill's nostrils; then he looked up at the rest of us, eyes big as saucers, like he just figured out what the rest of us already knew.

"Holy shit," he whispered.

Lester Johnson looked out the crummy window at the gray sky. The rain was coming down harder, going from a drizzle to something more like a cow pissing on a rock. "Well, you gotta hand it to him," Lester said. "Old Bill sure picked a prime day to permanently sleep in."

"So what do you want to do with him?" I asked. "Prop him up and hope Zeb don't notice?"

"Seems only fitting we leave him here," Crooked River said. "He has no family to claim him, and it wouldn't take long to bury him in this mud." Several heads nodded approval.

"What'll we do for a grave marker?" Luke asked. "A boulder for a headstone?"

"Leave that to me," I said.

Lester wandered outside long enough to make sure Zeb Walton, the crew boss, and Henry Longfellow, a state inspector, were still busy checking the first lines of trees. Then we carried old Bill on a blanket down the mountain in the opposite direction. We trudged carefully through the steep mud down the tree stump moonscape, stepping over rocks and deadfall past patches of snow and muddy streamlets. The air was so cold it could snap like a cucumber and it smelled salty like Pacific Ocean seaweed and tidal pools.

"This is good enough," Crooked River said, eyeing the spot where we stopped. We propped Old Bill up against a log and started on the grave, swinging hoedads in unison as the hole got bigger. Zeb was back at the crummy, hollering for us to quit cluster fucking and get back to work, but we still had twenty minutes on our lunch break, and we figured Zeb was being a pissant because he couldn't see us beyond the ridge.

We finally had a few good feet into the soil, smelling rich and mushroomy like humus and semen, and we rolled Old Bill in. Soon he was completely buried.

Then I did the last necessary thing. Swinging my hoedad hard, I parted the soil and Old Bill's rib cage clean to the ground beneath his back. You could hear the bones and cartilage cracking beneath the soil.

"Jee-zus!" Crooked River croaked.

"Calm down," I said. "You don't hear Old Bill complaining now, do you?" I widened the opening, picked up some long-rooted Douglas firs and planted them in Old Bill's heart. I had to reach down into that human flesh to make sure the trees didn't j-root; they were firm inside him, clean through, taproots protruding out his back, branches reaching up from his chest. There were five trees in all, and in time they would grow together into one massive tree.

The guys helped me brace a few rocks around the trees to give them a fighting chance, then we headed back up to the crummy, break over, picked up our packs - we already had hoedads in hand - and started back on our treelines.

All day I worked, and I dreamed a walking dream of how the great primeval stumps paid tribute to Old Bill as the forest we were planting row after row grew thick and strong, and salmon and trout splashed in the brooks, spotted owls nested in the branches, timber wolves howled and hunted in the shadows of the trees, ferns and moss and amanita muscaria and wayside asters and the wild Oregon grape and brackett fungi thrived, and as the five trees grew into one big granddaddy tree, Old Bill and his substance became a part of it, and deep down inside, I hoped and prayed that chainsaws and lumber jacks would never again work this part of the mountains, because you hate to see a good friend cut down like that, especially when he put his heart into his work.

SCHULTZ

TEA FOR THE SUNRISE

One day they found the few, fossilized bones of the first woman, and they named her Lucy, and, awed and puzzled, they asked her, "Why did your people die off? Why didn't they survive?" But Lucy asked back, across a bridge of millions of years, "And what makes you think your kind will survive?"

And will I survive? Donna Lane wondered at four in the morning as she crawled from her warm sleeping bag and out of the tent, bare hands on ice and rock until she stood, shivering beneath the inquiring stars. And will the sun last forever? Or will it burn itself out, leaving all life to starve to death?

She fumbled with her flashlight and her portable butane stove, struck a match and got the flame glowing cobalt blue, hissing coldly as she put a camper's pot full of water on it. Then she looked up, cold, her eyes full of the night's gems. And she thought about the pills.

The pills: her answer to what her life had become. She was now trying to be mother and father to her three, small children, still working, a bottle of wine every night to relax against the last few months of loneliness, dinners with canned creamed corn, mundane nights of eleven o'clock news and cigarettes and bills, and she kept telling herself: I'm not going to make it, I'm not going to make it . . .

Now, having had barely two hours of sleep, shivering and scared, she strapped the sharp-toothed steel crampons onto her hiking boots to complete her journey. Her tent was pitched just below Tabletop on Mount Adams in the state of Washington. It was her first, and last, mountain climb, and Mount Adams was, fortunately, not a technical climb that required ropes and pitons, though a rented ice axe and crampons helped. "You got more guts than I do," Maggie Wyles, who was watching her children that week, told her. But Donna knew it had nothing to do with courage. I'm scared, she thought, scared of living, and I'm lonely. So she brought the pills, because she had no intention of climbing back down the mountain.

Her twelve-year marriage with Matt came to mind as she watched the cold blue flame of the stove. A storybook romance, they grew up together, childhood sweethearts thriving symbiotically off each other, always working together, sharing laughs, traveling together, so very seldom apart. He was so kind, so encouraging when she began her career in realty two years ago.

Donna was intensely happy with her husband and her children. Then one night Matt flowered her over with talk of how much he loved her, and how he couldn't live without her, and the next day he went to work, never to return. He called her that evening from another woman's house, talking about separation and the quality of his life.

At the time, she didn't feel anything. She continued working, raising the children, attending those meetings of initials — MADD, NARAL, NOW. As though in a dream, she found herself heading into an affair with Steve Brecht, a songwriter and coworker, and she might have followed through with it had she not listened to three women from the office who casually chatted around a bar table about office affairs they had had with him. She felt even more alone than before.

And now she was on a mountain, wanting to die, the bottle of pills weighing heavily in her pocket. Though she worried about her children, and what effect her death would have on them, she knew her mother would raise them well. Though being on the mountain seemed irrational, she knew she couldn't die like Sylvia Plath, enclosed in a room, suffocated by gas. She needed freedom and a romantic death, because the romance of her life was gone.

It was almost four-thirty when Donna poured the hot, sugarless, lemon-grass tea into the thermos. Surrounded by ice and rock, her tent and the small blue flame from her stove became a sanctuary for her in the darkness. She gazed around, imagining a glacial age of mammoths and timber wolves, and fighting them off, she and the long-dead Neanderthal Lucy, with femur bones and rocks.

Glancing down toward the base of the mountain, she saw a caterpillaring line of lights, two dozen, maybe more, as though some stars had leaked from the sky and were trying to climb back up. They were flashlight-carrying climbers who, like her, were getting as early start. She didn't worry about it; the pills would finish their work long before another hiker would catch up with her.

Sighing, she braced herself against a boulder to urinate one last time, picked up her knapsack and ice axe, and began her ascension. The eastern horizon was already swirling, gray clouds, and soon it would be glowing red. For now, though, she used her flashlight, stepping carefully as a cold wind stabbed at her tear-damp cheeks.

Her breathing quickly became difficult, as though she were inhaling cream-of-mushroom soup, but that was to be expected in the thin air at ten thousand feet. Her crampons gripped ice and stone while her flashlight revealed details of the grayish landscape. Donna had hiked many times before, but she had never trained for a mountain climb. Her calves, still sore from the day before, now screamed with glass-sharp pain, and would be worse by the time she was done. But it didn't matter. Donna was escaping her own helplessness, pain or no pain.

A steep snowfield just east of the Suksdorf Ridge provided the best climbing, so she climbed there, kicking footholds into the snow, sometimes using the ice axe when snow became ice. She was no longer cold but sweating, having to stop every dozen steps to catch her breath. She glanced up at the stars, not so many visible now, as though they were reaching their extinction. The red of morning glowed beyond distant mountains like a swelling artery. Not once did she look back to watch the other climbers' progress.

She kept touching the bulging pocket with the bottle of pills. It both scared her and gave her strength. As she continued her ascent, she thought of the lyrics to one of Steve's songs: "The bear climbed to the top of a mountain . . . To watch a stream run down . . ." She also recalled Ernest Hemingway's story about finding the frozen, preserved carcass of a leopard on Mount Kilimanjaro, and how he wondered what it was doing at such a high altitude.

Donna's lungs now felt like shredded lettuce, and her calves and thighs felt like aching rubber bands, but she went on regardless. Suddenly long shadows leaped like striking snakes across per path. She glanced east, watching the sun peer over the mountains. Turning west, she saw Mount Saint Helens, twenty miles away, still sending up dust plumes a decade after the famous eruption.

Sighing, Donna turned off her flashlight and set it on a small ice ledge while she removed her knapsack to put it away. As she unzipped a pocket on her knapsack, the flashlight suddenly slipped and bounded down the steep slope. Donna pivoted and watched, feeling a sudden wave of vertigo as her new flashlight slid and bounced downhill. Only the lonely sound of each icy impact was audible over the moaning of the wind. Donna almost laughed; she felt deserted again. Watching the flashlight come to a stop a thousand feet downhill, she wondered about the ancient bones of Lucy. Did she die alone? she wondered. Was she a mother? Was she deserted, too? Donna squinted at the rising sun, her only witness. You, too, will make your circuit across the sky and desert me, too, she thought.

Her ascent continued, uneventful and slow. She reached the false summit of Mount Adams, walked the several hundred feet to the real summit, and climbed the last few hundred feet to the top in less than an hour, still gasping but barely aware of the pain in her lungs.

Having reached the top of the mountain, she was ready to take the pills she had planned to use for the last month, when she spotted the cabin. It was an old relic from the turn of the century, she recalled, that was supposed to be buried in snow, but now, most of the roof and part of one wall were visible, reminding Donna of Noah's Ark on Mount Ararat. She walked over to the ancient, cedar-shingled roof and noticed a flat, rectangular aluminum box just inside a window. Pulling it out and opening it, she found a register inside. There were pages and pages filled with names of those who reached the top, and several whittled pencils awaiting more names.

Donna thought of the line of climbers as hour or so behind her. She thought of the pills, knowing they would finish their job before the other climbers reached her. Moving almost mechanically, she unshouldered her knapsack as she recalled the story of the cabin. Two men had constructed it, using mules to haul large logs to the top of the mountain. They were apparently mining sulfur. They are long-dead now, Donna thought, but they didn't climb Mount Adams to die. Neither did the leopard climb Mount Kilimanjaro to die. And Lucy, in her quest for her mountain, wasn't seeking death either.

Donna felt her courage waning. With shaking hands, she unzipped her knapsack and pulled out the thermos. Sitting on the bone-gray shingles of the roof, she unscrewed the plastic cup from the thermos, thinking about her children. She fully realized how selfish her dying was, and what a nightmarish legacy she was leaving behind for them, but her own pain outweighed her maternal instincts. She was not the kind of person who could replace the lifetime love of a spouse with the needful love of her children. She had a void in her life, deep, painful, permanent.

Robot-like, she removed the lid from the thermos and poured out a cupful of brown amber tea, the steam rising in the early morning sunlight, only to be blown away by the icy wind. She knew she would have to work fast, while she had the courage. She removed the pill bottle from her pocket, poured some pills into the palm of her hand, and in one quick motion, her eyes wide, her hands shaking, she dropped them onto the ground, stomping them into the snow with her crampon-wielding boots, pouring the rest of the pills onto those, then scraping snow over them with her ice axe. Until the moment she saw the register, she never realized how much she wanted to survive.

Once again, she recalled the bones; Lucy was dead, and her race of people was gone, but surely they fought hard to survive. Donna glanced east. The sun was high above the mountain, high in a light blue cloudless sky. The sun, always deserting her, but always coming back. And she thought about her children, and how they would have a better chance of survival if she went home.

Having reached the summit of Mount Adams, intending to sign the register, she knew now that she would be surviving, she would go home, pain and all, to overcome other mountains. She lifted her cup, no longer tea of death, but tea for the sunrise, tea for life and a new beginning. She took a sip and thought about a bear that watched a stream run down.

FIVE   1/197   T. NEWTON SCHULTZ

CREDITS

Eleven Roses	**The Florida Times-Union (December 23, 1989) (2nd Place, Christmas Story Contest Florida Times-Union)**
Tuesday's Scenario	**Writer's Open Forum (January, 1993)**
The Man Who Lived In The Cellar	**The Endeavour (January, 1993) Popular Fiction By Oregon Authors (Anthology) (1986)**
Beaver Attack	**The Endeavour (April, 1995)**
Grandfather Carp	**Puck And Pluck (1991)**
Listing	**Experiments In Words (1991)**
Calling	**Cerberus (August, 1997)**

Planting

**Phoenix Rising
(November, 1995)**

**Tea For The Sunrise Renegade
(1994)**

FIVE   1/197   T. NEWTON SCHULTZ